For those who treat their time on this Earth as a privilege
instead of a right, may we share the responsibility.

The Wish of Wishes by Liam Snead
Illustrations and cover design by Madeleine Kunda

Lizard Head Publishing
319 Adams Ranch Road 1102
Telluride, CO 81435

www.lizardheadpublishing.com

ISBN 978-1-7355960-3-7

Printed in the U.S.A.

The Wish of Wishes

Written by Liam Snead

Illustrated by Madeleine Kunda

izard Head Publishing

One starry night, on Christmas Eve, not too long ago,
a polar bear came walking by, through the winter snow.
From where he came the little fox knew she could not say,
but judging by his tired look, he'd traveled through the day.

"Don't be scared," said the bear as the fox began to shake.
"For I am just a cub like you. A kid, for goodness sake!
I wouldn't dream of eating such a little fox as you.
To make a friend, such as yourself, is what I'd rather do."

"Are you lost?" the fox then asked. "You seem so far from home.
I've never known a polar bear to come this way to roam.
A walrus, sure, and puffins too. Now and then a fish."
The bear just smiled, then he said, "I'm off to make a wish.

"I'm on my way, this Christmas Eve, to look for Santa's shop.
I've had a tip it's up the hill, nearly at the top.
I'm sure the elves are working hard through their evening shift.
I hope that Santa has the time to give a bear a gift."

"I can't believe it!" cried the fox, jumping in the air.
"For I am going there as well, to get some Christmas care.
I've got a Christmas wish to make. A special wish, oh yes.
Far more special than your own, if I had to guess."

"We'll see 'bout that," laughed the bear, picking up his paws.
"Come along and join me as I look for Santa Claus!"
Off they went, two little ones in search of journey's end.
Side by side they trotted off, each glad to find a friend.

Part way up the slope they stopped, most surprised to see
a seal was caught up in the snow, as stuck as he could be.
"I'm much too small to eat!" he said. "Please just pass me by."
He hid his eyes beneath his flippers, trying not to cry.

"We're not a threat," Bear and Fox heartily assured.
"We wouldn't hurt a fellow pup. It's true, you have our word.
We're headed to the mountaintop, searching for St. Nick.
You can join us if you like. We swear it's not a trick."

The seal pup smiled, most relieved, and sighed a little sigh.
"I'm glad to hear that others have the same desire as I.
My Christmas wish might be the most important wish of all,
so I've been climbing up this hill, trying not to fall."

The bear and fox stepped up and said, "Now we've got your back."
They pulled their new friend from the snow and got him back on track.
"There's not much time," said the bear, as he took the lead.
"Christmas Day is coming fast, and there's three things we need."

Up and up and up they climbed, puffing as they went.
By the time they reached the top, all three friends were spent.
"My oh my!" they gave a shout, for right before their eyes,
there was Santa's twinkling palace, reaching toward the skies.

"We made it!" cried the polar bear. "At last!" exclaimed the seal.
"I hope he'll see us," said the fox. "I hope he strikes a deal."
They walked along the snowy path, past the reindeer shack,
following the sign that said, "The shop's around the back."

In the back they came across a nervous-looking elf,
reading from a paper list, mumbling to himself.
"One hundred dolls, and building blocks, and ninety-five toy planes.
Not to mention eighty cases of those model trains."

"Pardon me," said the bear. The little elf jumped up!
"I'm sure you've got a busy night, we hate to interrupt.
The three of us have traveled far, hardly taking pause.
I wonder, could you tell us where we might find Santa Claus?"

Though he heard every word, the elf could not believe.
"Santa Claus?" he scoffed. "Don't you know it's Christmas Eve?
Santa's busy as can be. He's loading up his sleigh.
He hasn't got the time for you. Come back another day."

"We can't come back," explained the fox. "It's got to be tonight.
We have to talk to Santa now, before he makes his flight."
"We've got three wishes," said the seal.
"We simply must insist."
The elf then rolled his eyes and said,
"Just put them on the list."

Handing them his lengthy scroll,
they each wrote down a wish.
When they'd finished with the
page, he took it with a swish.
"Can Santa do it?" asked the fox.
"Can he change his plan?"
"We'll see," replied the tiny elf.
"He's quite a busy man."

But glancing down upon the list,
the elf stopped in his tracks.
His eyes had finished reading, then
widened to the max.
"Three gifts, indeed!" he said aloud.
"Important wishes, true!
Follow me with greatest speed,
I'll see what I can do."

Then he led them through the workshop, where they stopped in awe.
The twinkling lights were the brightest that they ever saw!
Stacks of toys and Christmas gifts were piled to the ceiling,
giving them the tingles of a warm and happy feeling.

Elves were working everywhere, trying to beat the clock.

Their tools were spread across the room, so it was hard to walk.

Hammers banged and sawdust swirled like evening winter snow.

The wrapping section made sure every present had a bow.

Then the wee elf took them to a magic elevator.

"Name your level, if you please," said the operator.

"Take us straight up to the top!" said the elf with haste.

"They've got to see old Santa Claus, without a moment's waste."

Up and up and up they went,
to the palace roof.

Then the lift doors opened wide
with a sudden "poof!"

There was Santa's flying sleigh,
big, and packed, and steady.

All the reindeer stood up front,
alert and at the ready.

"Follow me!" said the elf,
looking full of cheer.

"I think we made it just in time.
Santa's at the rear."

Walking fast, the whole group knew
they had no time to spare,

but then a reindeer blocked their path, saying,
"Stop right there!"

"Come on, Dasher!" cried the elf.
"Don't make such a fuss.
These three must see
Santa Claus. No time to discuss."
"Clear the runway," said the
reindeer. "Now it's time to leave.
Santa told us that we have to
start our Christmas Eve."

Pretty soon the elf and reindeer got into a spat.
The polar bear and fox and seal were worried about that.
The thought of missing Santa Claus had filled them with much fear,
but suddenly a voice behind them said, "What have we here?"

Turning 'round, they saw a woman standing in the snow.

Mrs. Claus, they knew she was, without her saying so.

She smiled a smile as warm as all the cookies on her plate.

"No need to fight," she kindly said. "My husband's going to wait.

"Every year on Christmas Eve he craves for something sweet.

He won't be leaving in his sleigh until he's had a treat."

The little bear, the fox, and seal all quivered with delight,

as she took them to the man   they'd hoped to see all night.

Standing tall and putting one last sack upon his sleigh,
there was jolly Santa Claus, set for Christmas day.
Looking down, he smiled to see his three well-traveled guests.
"They've come quite far," said the elf. "They've come with three requests."

"Ho ho hello!" laughed old St. Nick. "You've caught me just in time.
I'm off to make the evening rounds before the midnight chime.
But tell me now, my little friends, what can I do for you?
I'll happily grant your wishes, making them come true."

The polar bear then took his time, careful with each word.
And then the fox cleared her throat, anxious to be heard.
And then the seal considered why he'd set off all alone.
Then all at once the three friends said, "Dear Santa, save my home."

Surprise, surprise! How far they'd walked, not knowing that they came
for very special wishes that turned out to be the same.
Santa, and the tiny elf, and dear old Mrs. C.
listened closely as the little wishers made their plea.

"Ice is quickly melting, winter days are growing warm."
"All around us homes are changing, starting to transform."
"So we came from far away, just to see your face,
and make a wish this Christmas Eve for a safer place."

Santa Claus looked as if he knew not what to say.
The merry twinkle in his eye had seemed to fade away.
"My friends, I fear you've made a wish I cannot guarantee.
For this is a rare kind of wish that isn't up to me.

"One person cannot promise to make this wish come true,
but maybe there's a simple thing that you and I can do.
One smallest hope perhaps could make the Earth a little better,
so write the children of the world a Merry Christmas Letter."

Then he beckoned to the elf, "Will you please transcribe?
You see, my friends, he'll scribble down each thing that you describe.
Speak your hearts, taking care to mean each word you say.
I'll leave this letter for each child to have
on Christmas day."

And so the bear and fox and seal put their heads together.
Speaking from their deepest hearts, they made a Christmas letter.
As they worked, Mrs. Claus made sure to bring them snacks.
In the end, the elf sealed up the note with candle wax.

When they'd finished, Santa bid them all a fond goodbye.
"Merry Christmas to you all! Now it's time to fly!"
Off he went, leaving with the reindeer and his sleigh.
Hearts aglow, all the others watched him fly away.

"Now, my friends," said Mrs. Claus. "There's much we get for hopin.'
If you ever need a home, our doors are always open."
The furry friends, knowing that this Christmas Eve was fateful,
wrapped the lady in a hug, feeling warm and grateful.

Christmas morning dawned upon the world with happy light.
Boys and girls from everywhere awoke with great delight.
Sure enough, on every pile of presents could be seen
a letter written gracefully in ink of red and green.

To the children of the world,
A happy holiday!

We hope you'll take a little time to read these words we say.
We've reached the portion of the year that comes with care and giving.
Today we cherish all the things that make a life worth living.

Morning sun. Sparkling rain. A cool evening breeze.
The colors of the autumn leaves dancing in the trees.
A shelter to rest your head as winds begin to blow.
A family that holds you tight through the winter snow.

We smile to think about the joy of all you girls and boys,
waking up to greet the day, unwrapping all your toys.
Yet every year, on Christmas Day, we hope that you will ponder
all the creatures of the world and all the lands they wander.

Christmas time is not just for the gifts that we are given.
It's a time to make the world the place we'd like to live in.
Maybe, if we try to keep this spirit through the year,
every day can be like Christmas, filled with joy and cheer.

Looking past our differences, there's so much we can do.
The three of us can now be friends, so maybe you can too!
Together, we can work to make this wish of wishes real.

Sending all our peace and love,

Bear & Fox & Seal